My Little Pony

THE MAGICAL MUSIC BOX

Applejack crept quietly through the orchard. "Apple sauce," she whispered, "I wish the moon would come out from behind the clouds. I can't see where I'm going, or where I've been, and I do want to find my favourite apple tree."

Just then, Applejack heard a strange swishing sound and a little white shape appeared in front of her. "Pony feathers!" wailed Applejack. "It's a ghost!"

"Don't be silly, Applejack. It's me, Rowena the moonbeam."

Rowena laughed as she danced in front of the pony, and suddenly the orchard glowed with a silvery light.

"Here's my favourite tree," smiled Applejack, stretching her neck to reach a rosy apple. "Mmm, this is good. Would you like one, Rowena?"

The little moonbeam shook her head. "You know I only eat moon food. I am hungry though. I'll just deliver this present to Medley then I'll go for my supper. I can hear the Man in the Moon calling me."

"I'll stay here for a while and finish my supper," said Applejack.

Rowena visited many different lands through the night and was often given parcels to deliver. Smiling down at the sleeping pony, Rowena placed a gaily wrapped parcel by Medley's side. "I do wish I could see her face when she opens it," she whispered to herself.

Medley was excited when she woke up and saw the parcel. "I must go and find the other ponies," she said. "They'll be at the Waterfall," and as she flew from cloud to cloud, Medley sang happily:

"A present for me, a present for me,
 I just wonder what it can be.
 It is not big, it's something small,
 And here I am at the Waterfall."

"Medley's got a present," called Firefly,
performing a treble backward loop.

"I can't wait to see what it is," laughed Medley, as she and Firefly landed together.

Sprinkles hurried from underneath the Waterfall, covering the grass with frothy bubbles.

"Pony feathers!" cried Sparkler, as she ran to join them. "Don't spoil the wrapping paper, Sprinkles, it's got silver stars on it."

"And you would like the stars for your collection?" said Medley, handing the wrapping paper to Sparkler.

"What's inside?" called Baby Glory, splashing out of the water. "Hurry up and look, Medley."

"It's a box," said Sprinkles, as Medley lifted it out. "Open the lid, Medley."

As Medley lifted the lid, music filled the air. "A music box!" she exclaimed. "What a lovely present! I wonder who sent it?"

"Ask Rowena," said Applejack, but nobody heard her for they were too busy dancing. Even the Rainbow seemed to be swaying in time to the music.

Only Sparkler was still. She was watching the tiny jewelled pony shape twirling around the top of the music box. "Oh, I do wish I could see it properly," she thought. "I could design a shape like that for my collection."

Sometimes the music would stop for a while, then a new tune started to play.

"Let's play musical stepping stones," suggested Sprinkles. "Whenever the music stops I'll blow some bubbles. You must catch one and run to a stepping stone. If the bubble bursts before you get there, you're out."

Baby Surprise gave a sudden giggle. When the music stopped again she made a tiny little balloon. Baby Glory, thinking it was a bubble, caught it.

"You're out, Baby Glory," shouted Sprinkles. "That's a balloon you've caught."

Baby Glory laughed and lay down to watch the others play. "The music box is just like magic," she thought sleepily. "I do wish I could see how it works."

The ponies danced and played until midday, when it was time to go to Dream Castle for lunch.

"Majesty, just look at my present," said Medley after lunch. "It's a music box; I'll make it play for you." But when Medley opened the box, nothing happened.

Spike, the little dragon, tugged Majesty's tail urgently.

"It's all right Spike," Majesty said gently, "I know where we've seen this music box before."

She looked round anxiously, then made a strange sound. At once she was surrounded by all the little ponies in Pony Land. "Who is missing?" she asked. "Sparkler and Baby Glory. Anyone else?"

"No, everyone else is here," called Cotton Candy, who loved counting.

Majesty twirled her magic horn. Suddenly, a strange figure arrived by her side. "Magician Muddle, is this your music box?" asked Majesty.

"Yes! Where did you find it? It is three times full of bad magic, for it was a spell that went wrong. You and Spike saw the box when you came to visit me. I kept it locked up."

"Somebody must have unlocked it . . ." began Majesty.

"Anyway, it doesn't matter," interrupted the magician. "I have worked out a spell to unmuddle the bad magic. What a good job the box has been found in time."

"I'm afraid it hasn't been found in time," sighed Majesty. "The music will not play any more, and that means the bad magic has been used."

"Great fire-eating dragons!" shouted Spike impatiently. "Sparkler and Baby Glory are missing. Unmuddle the spell, Magician Muddle."

"It's three times full of bad magic," repeated the magician. "Something must have happened that you don't know about. I can't do the spell until I know what the third thing is."

"Medley, who gave you the music box?" asked Majesty.

"It was Rowena," said Applejack. "I told you once, but you . . ."

"Never mind all that!" yelled the magician. "Find me something belonging to the missing ponies and Rowena, or something they touched recently."

Baby Surprise gave the magician a balloon. "Baby Glory was playing with it," she gasped.

Firefly flew away and returned with a glitter shape from Sparkler's collection.

"Rowena touched me last night," said Applejack. "But we don't know if she is missing so why do you need something she touched?"

"I used moonbeam dust in the spell that got muddled," said the magician, running his hands over Applejack's back.

"The dust will have grown into a moonbeam inside the music box. The moonbeam must have tried to reach Rowena but the bad magic wouldn't let it out."

"Why did Rowena bring the box to me?" asked Medley.

"Your name was on the wrapping paper. Before the spell got muddled and bad, the music box was going to be a present for you."

"You're unmuddling the bad spell," shouted Spike. "Look!"

"*Those inside to their proper size, music box go, before our eyes,*" shouted the magician.

There was a loud bang and the music box disappeared. Sparkler, Baby Glory, Rowena and a small moonbeam blinked as they looked around.

"Did you make wishes? Is that how you got inside the box?" the magician asked.

"Yes," gasped Baby Glory. "But we'll never make another wish."

"Oh, you will," laughed the magician. "Now I've found the right spell, I'm going to make a wishing music box for everyone."

"Not today," laughed Majesty. "I've just made a party spell. Come on everybody, into the castle."